DOCTOR · WHO

DECIDE YOUR DESTINY

BBC CHILDREN'S BOOKS
Published by the Penguin Group
Penguin Books Ltd, 80 Strand, London, WC2R 0RL, England
Penguin Group (USA) Inc., 375 Hudson Street, New York, New York 10014, USA
Penguin Books (Australia) Ltd, 250 Camberwell Road, Camberwell, Victoria 3124, Australia
(A division of Pearson Australia Group Pty Ltd)
Canada, India, New Zealand, South Africa
Published by BBC Children's Books, 2007
Text and design © Children's Character Books, 2007
Written by Richard Dungworth
10 9 8 7 6 5 4 3 2 1
ISBN-13: 978-1-40590-381-3
ISBN-10: 1-40590-381-3
Printed in Great Britain by Clays Ltd, St Ives plc

DOCTOR · WHO

DECIDE YOUR DESTINY

The Crystal Snare

by Richard Dungworth

The Crystal Snare

1 | '**K**eep going, Martha! Something's coming through!'

As you slowly surface from a strange dream of clinging hands and ghostly lights, an unfamiliar voice reaches you over the rush of blood in your ears.

'Blimey, Doctor — it's a kid!'

This second voice is female, and too real to belong to your fast-fading dream.

You open your eyes. You are no longer in bed, in your room. Instead you are lying on an uncomfortable hammock of thin steel rope. Above you, a complex apparatus of cogs, levers and spinning copper arms whirs busily.

Two people you have never seen before are enthusiastically working a double set of foot-treadles connected by a drive belt to the peculiar contraption. The man is dressed in an unlikely combination of pinstriped suit and baseball sneakers. His companion is in her twenties, pretty, with a lively spark behind her brown eyes. As they step down from the treadles, the gyrating arms above you start to slow.

'I knew I could get it working! A nineteenth-century time machine — how about that, Martha? The amazing thing is that whoever put this little beauty together was on the right track. All I had to do was add a couple of temporal flux stabilisers, make the odd tweak here and there with the old sonic screwdriver, and Bob's your uncle — treadle-powered time travel!'

He pulls a slim silver tool from his pocket, moves to where two small electronic devices are clamped to the clockwork contraption, and begins removing them.

'Best leave things as we found them, eh? Don't think the Victorians are quite ready for Time Lord technology. They're still pretty giddy about steam power.'

The woman has noticed your bewildered look. She approaches, smiling warmly.

'Hi. I'm Martha. Nice PJs. Guess you're wondering what's going on.'

You nod as she helps you from the strange hammock.

'Well, the Doctor here,' — Martha casts her companion a withering look — 'couldn't resist dropping in on this famous Victorian event, to have a drool over all the old machines.' She leans closer, pretending to whisper. 'Bit of a techno-geek, he is.'

'Oh, come on, Martha,' replies the Doctor. 'This is the greatest exhibition of human technology and art the Earth has ever seen. *Such* a great exhibition, in fact, they called it just that – The Great Exhibition.'

'Anyhow,' continues Martha, 'I bet the Doctor he couldn't get this "Temporal Translator" contraption – it's one of the exhibits – working. Challenged him to "translate" something from my own time. But I said some*thing*, not some*one*!'

The Doctor looks shifty.

'Mmm, yes... *minor* miscalculation, I'll admit. But not to worry!'

He crosses to a nearby railing. As you and Martha join him, you find yourself looking out over a truly breathtaking scene. You are on a gallery that overlooks the interior of a vast cathedral-like hall. Its nave stretches away as far as you can see. And the entire building appears to be made of glass.

'Magnificent, isn't it?' says the Doctor. 'The Crystal Palace. Designed by ex-gardener Joseph Paxton, specifically to house the Exhibition. Almost 300,000 panes of glass and over 4,000 tons of ironwork, all put together here in London's Hyde Park in less than four months.'

The area of the gallery immediately around you is occupied by all kinds of weird and wonderful devices. A banner above it reads PHILOSOPHICAL INSTRUMENTS. Below you, the nave's central avenue is similarly brimming with an astonishing variety of exhibits.

'The Works of Industry of All Nations,' says the Doctor. 'Over 100,000 items from nearly 14,000 international exhibitors. This was one of the most ambitious undertakings of Queen Victoria's reign — the brainchild of her darling husband, Prince Albert. It was a runaway success, too. Over *six million* visitors. If you were around in 1851, this was *the* main event.'

He flashes you an infectious grin.

'And as it's a Sunday, we've got the entire place to ourselves — well, except for a police constable or two. Come on — let's take a look around.'

To start by exploring the Philosophical Instruments section, go to 93. To take the nearby staircase down to the ground floor, go to 57.

2 The nanobotic creatures come scuttling down from the cotton mill's overhead workings. Reaching the floor, they also split up — one hurrying after Martha as the other comes after you.

You flee through the Machinery in Motion section, entering an area crammed with gleaming machine tools: powerful lathes, planing and shaping machines, slotting and drilling machines, and punching and shearing machines. These are the creations of Joseph Whitworth, the nineteenth-century's finest machine tool manufacturer.

Several of the large machines are active — clearly Brunel has already managed to get them under steam. The nearest is a huge lathe, used for cutting steel wheels for the fast-expanding Victorian railways.

You halt, breathless, and turn to see whether you have shaken off your robotic enemy. But it is still on your tail.

To charge at the creature, and try to push it backwards into the spinning jaws of the steam lathe, go to 42. To keep running, go to 17.

3 By surrendering to the nanobotic creatures, you buy yourself a little time. You are now in their power — but at least you're alive.

The creatures escort you and the Doctor roughly along the tunnel, until it opens into a large chamber. The chamber's walls are coated with the same luminous green substance that lines the tunnel. A large, transparent, cylindrical pod occupies the centre of the floor. Inside it you can see fifty or so human beings, each enclosed within a capsule of blue gel.

'Of *course*!'

The Doctor confronts the creatures.

'You're Shryken reconnaissance, aren't you? An advance sampling party. I knew I recognised the technology.'

He turns back to you.

'The Shryken have a long history of planetary invasion, always with the same strategy. Send in a remote-controlled reconnaissance probe manned with nanobots, to abduct a sample of the population. When the probe ship returns with the sample specimens, the Shryken perform a biological analysis on them. Then they bioengineer a virus to exploit one of the native race's weaknesses. Knocks out the entire population, without any need for conflict, leaving the planet there for the taking.'

He turns again to his nanobotic guard.

'And the Great Exhibition offers the ideal sampling pool, doesn't it? Humans from all nations, in all their biological diversity. The Shryken must have landed the remote ship near the Crystal Palace, then had you burrow this tunnel network underneath it. From here, you can enter the exhibition as replicant policemen, and pick off visitors one at a time.'

He looks across at the cylindrical pod, in which a single gel capsule lies empty.

'Looks like they wanted Martha to complete their sample. My guess is they're preparing the probe ship for the return voyage any time now.'

The creatures herd you and the Doctor across the chamber to the far wall. An opening appears in the rock, and you are shoved through it, into a cramped cell. In one corner, looking dishevelled but defiant, sits Martha. As the door slices shut behind you, the Doctor returns her relieved embrace.

You can hear the creatures outside moving away, clearly content that you are securely imprisoned.

To attempt to force the doorway open, go to 71. To wait while the Doctor tries his sonic screwdriver on it, go to 52.

4 As you hurry away, a loud clattering fills the air. The policeman has spotted you, and is urgently operating a hand-held alarm that looks and sounds like an old-fashioned football rattle.

'Run for it!'

The Doctor leads you and Martha in a dash along the nave's central avenue, past one impressive exhibit after another: a fifteen-metre-long model of Liverpool docks; a massive lighthouse reflector mechanism; a bronze statue of a bowman shooting an eagle, encased in a towering cast iron dome.

You pull up just beyond this, breathless. There's no sign of pursuit.

'This bit's for "British Possessions Overseas",' says the Doctor, taking in your surroundings. He gives a wry smile. 'Countries that "belong" to the British Crown. Victoria's Empire covered nearly a quarter of the planet.'

He gestures to the banners above the two nearest display areas, on which are embroidered the words AUSTRALIA and AFRICA.

'Pick a colony!'

To explore the Australian section, go to 21.
To choose Africa, go to 62.

5 To your relief, the danger passes. You emerge from your hiding place and continue your tour. As you and the Doctor admire more bizarre mechanical inventions, Martha tuts impatiently.

'You're gadget-mad, you two!'

She peers hopefully along the gallery.

'The next section looks like nineteenth-century medicines and stuff. Could be good for my medical training.' And she hurries ahead.

The Doctor is examining an odd box-shaped contraption. A plaque beside it reads:

Carpenter and Westley's Improved
PHANTASMAGORIA LANTERN
With the Chromatrope and Dissolving views

The Doctor slots a glass plate into the machine. As he winds a handle at the back, a flickering image is projected on to a white cloth screen a short distance away.

'Excellent! Victorian home cinema! Hard to believe that human technology will move from this to DVD in only 150 years. Go on — try another slide…'

To try out the Phantasmagoria Lantern, go to 13. To catch up with Martha in the Pharmaceuticals section, go to 68.

6 Before you can come up with a solution, the Doctor bursts through the door of the chamber. With a quick sweep of his sonic screwdriver, he seals it behind him.

'They're not... far... behind...' he pants, hurrying to join you, Martha and Brunel. With a few more deft movements of the sonic, he releases the wrist and ankle restraints.

As Brunel flexes his freed limbs, the Doctor's face lights up with recognition.

'Well, well — the century's finest engineer! Loved your Clifton Suspension Bridge. *Great* middle name, too!'

Something crashes violently against the sealed door.

'Quick!' urges the Doctor. 'The Transmat portal!' He rushes to the far end of the chamber, where a diamond-shape of absolute blackness hangs impossibly in mid-air. Stepping into it, he vanishes.

You, Martha and Brunel quickly follow, and find yourselves back in the nave of the Crystal Palace — in the British Possessions Overseas section.

'Glad to be out of *there,*' gasps Martha. 'But what was that pod full of people, Doctor? Who's imprisoned them like that?'

'The Shryken. Or rather their nanobotic research party. They're empire builders, like your dear Queen Victoria. When they're planning a planetary invasion, they send in a reconnaissance probe first. Carries an advance party of robotic remotes — the nanobots — whose job is to abduct a sample of the population. When the probe returns, the Shryken use the sample specimens to draw up a biological profile of the natives. Then they manufacture an appropriate virus to wipe them out. No need for engagement of any kind. Very efficient.'

The Doctor gestures to the glass hall around you.

'They must have seen the Exhibition as an ideal sampling pool — people from all over the Earth. They had the nanobots burrow beneath it, replace the security police with replicants, then start picking off visitors.'

He turns to Brunel.

'We'll need power to fight them. What have we got to work with?'

'There's a boiler room at the north-east end,' replies Brunel. 'It supplies the steam-powered machinery through under-floor pipes. I can try to reach that, and get pressure up to run the machines.'

'Good man.'

As Brunel hurries away, the Doctor turns back to you and Martha.

'We better get a move on, too. That door won't hold for long.'

To move off through the Canadian section, go to 18. To enter the area displaying exhibits from the Bahamas and Trinidad, go to 50.

7 In the Agricultural section, alongside basic nineteenth-century farming equipment — scythes, hoes, hay-forks, simple horse-drawn ploughs — you find examples of more sophisticated, up-to-the-minute machinery.

'The Industrial Revolution is triggering an agricultural one,' explains the Doctor, admiring a complex contraption labelled:

GARRETT'S IMPROVED THRESHING MACHINE

'Increased mechanisation means one man can do the work of many. McCormick's Mechanical Reaper — over in the American section — is one of the exhibition's big hits. It'll change farming forever.'

Martha gives a sudden gasp. A police constable is making his way towards you through the agricultural exhibits. The Doctor, unfazed, pulls what looks like a blank piece of paper from his pocket, and strides to meet him.

'Morning, constable. Cornelius Garrett, of Garrett and Sons. My associates and I are preparing the exhibits for tomorrow's visitors.'

To stand your ground, in the hope that the Doctor's bluff works, go to 10. To run for it, go to 73.

Even as you pause to think, a snake-like tentacle whips out from the hole and coils around you. You struggle to prise it off, but its grip is formidable. Despite your resistance, you are hauled down into the blackness.

After a few heartbeats of complete darkness, you emerge in a wide underground tunnel. Luminous green ribs reinforce its rock walls. By their eerie light, you can see that the replicant policemen you were following have now transformed. Both have become cybernetic monstrosities, each with a dozen thrashing tentacles. You are in the grasp of one of these nanobotic monsters. The Doctor, close by, is bravely attempting to fight off the other.

The crushing tentacle around your chest is making it impossible to breathe. If you don't break free in the next few seconds, you're going to pass out.

To continue to struggle against your captor's grip, go to 14. To stop resisting, in the hope that surrender might increase your chance of survival, go to 3.

9 It seems an eternity before the Doctor returns — only to tell you that he has had no luck tracking down the TARDIS.

'I was counting on using some spare components to put together a surprise for our nanobotic friends,' he complains. 'If there's no TARDIS to work with, we'll have to see what else we can lay our hands on.'

He looks thoughtful for a moment.

'There's not much to be had in the 1850s by way of electronic stuff — electricity is still considered a bit new-fangled. But I bet they have some of Samuel Morse's telegraphic equipment on show. It's a major innovation in communications — they laid the first cross-channel cable only last year. If we can find out where the telegraph machines are, there might be a few bits and bobs I can use...'

To split up to look for the telegraph machines, go to 91. To seek them together, go to 49.

The coldness behind the police constable's stare gives you the distinct feeling that the Doctor's bluff isn't going to work.

'My authorisation by Her Majesty's Commissioners is here in print,' perseveres the Doctor. 'I can assure you…'

His voice trails off, as something unsettling begins to happen. The police constable appears to be melting. His top hat, facial features, high coat collars — all in turn are rapidly dissolving into a dark, fluid mass that flows down to the wooden floor, forming a spreading black pool.

As you watch, mystified, the Doctor reaches out and clutches a fistful of the constable's fast-dissolving chest. When he opens his hand, a small black mass writhes on his palm. Although its movement is fluid, it isn't wet, like a puddle of liquid. Instead, it is made up of countless tiny dry granules, like black sand. It slithers from the Doctor's hand to pour into the expanding pool around the vanishing policeman's feet.

'No wonder the psychic paper didn't work — you're not human at all, are you?' murmurs the Doctor. 'You're a nanobotic replica!'

His brow creases in a frown.

'But who's controlling you?'

By now, there is nothing left of the policeman's human form. But something else is beginning to take shape from the pool of black matter. As the three of you instinctively back away, Martha tugs at the Doctor's arm.

'What do you mean, "nanobotic", Doctor?'

'That thing's a machine, a cybernetic appliance made up from millions of microscopic robotic units — nanobots. They can combine and cooperate in an infinite number of forms — in this case a fake human policeman.'

The dry pool has now almost half-vanished, shaped within moments into an altogether different entity — a black, insectoid form. The mantis-like creature advances, clicking its sharp mandibles menacingly. As it does so, a second nanobotic monster rises rapidly from the remainder of the pool.

To stand your ground, go to 78. To run for it, go to 30.

11 | The area you now enter, adjoining the daguerreotype section, is dedicated to other forms of printing and early photography. It includes examples of the prints themselves, and the equipment used to create them.

One display illustrates the process of chromolithography — an invention that has recently generated the first colour prints. There are also examples of early calotypes — photographs on paper — as well as a collection of fine engravings.

You are looking at a display of stereotypes — cast metal plates used for printing multiple copies — when a top-hatted police constable suddenly strides from behind a nearby cabinet. Seeing you, the policeman halts, and begins to dissolve into a mass of nanobots. They rapidly recombine in the form of a ghastly, multi-limbed creature.

To arm yourself with one of the heavy stereotype printing plates, and confront your enemy, go to 63. To run for it, go to 17.

The distraction of Martha's scream gives the nanobotic monster a chance to recover. Lunging forward, it lands a powerful blow on the Doctor's jaw, sending him sprawling. But as you brace yourself for its next strike, it unexpectedly lumbers backwards.

You watch, puzzled, as the creature traces a large diamond in thin air with one of its foreclaws. As it completes the outline, eerie green light fills the diamond shape. It is as though the creature has cut a window in the air, and the strange light is spilling through it.

The creature launches itself through this impossible window, and vanishes.

You hurry to help the Doctor. He is alive, but badly dazed. He manages a weak nod towards the diamond window.

'Transmat portal...' he murmurs, eyes bleary. 'Door... where they're coming from... find Martha... careful... might be shielded... stun you...'

Then he blacks out.

To attempt to follow the creature through the Transmat portal, go to 14. To go after Martha, go to 46.

The magic lantern is charming. You and the Doctor try a selection of slides, until Martha returns from the Pharmaceutical section. She is carrying an armful of medicine bottles.

'Look at these, you two.'

The labels make interesting reading:

CROSBY'S INFALLIBLE LINIMENT
DR COBDEN'S BALSAMIC COUGH ELIXIR
HEMSLEY'S WORM-DESTROYING SYRUP
BLOOD PURIFYING VEGETABLE PILLS

The Doctor smiles, then claps his hands decisively.

'Right — time to sample the delights of the ground floor...'

As he hurries to the nearby staircase, you and Martha follow. But at its foot, you come face to face with another tall, blue-coated police constable. The Doctor is first to react, quickly producing what looks like a blank piece of paper from his pocket.

'Ah, Constable. Good. Albert Crump esquire, of Crump and Frottling, cleaners of distinction. My colleagues and I are inspecting the quality of the floor-polishing.'

He smiles disarmingly.

To stand your ground and hope the Doctor's bluff works, go to 10. To run for it, go to 73.

14 Your head swims sickeningly. As you slowly regain consciousness, your vision clears. You are bewildered to find yourself in a large underground chamber, pinned against its cold rock wall by restraints around your wrists and ankles. The chamber is eerily lit by the glow of a peculiar fluorescent resin that coats its walls and ceiling.

'Are you OK?'

Your relief at hearing Martha's voice is short-lived — she is in the same predicament as you, secured to the wall a few metres away. You nod, then ask her where on Earth you are.

An unfamiliar male voice answers.

'We are below the Crystal Palace. The police-creatures brought us all here.'

You twist your head awkwardly to see a third prisoner beyond Martha — a forty-something Victorian gentleman.

Martha introduces the stranger. 'This is Mr Brunel. Isambard Kingdom Brunel. The famous engineer.'

Brunel nods his head towards the centre of the chamber, indicating a large transparent cylindrical pod that lies there. Inside it you can see the bodies of around fifty human beings. Each is unconscious, enclosed in a gel-filled capsule.

'The others have been rendered senseless and incarcerated in that device, for some purpose,' says Brunel.

At the far end of the pod, three capsules stand empty.

'I believe we may be next...'

To attempt to wrestle free of your bonds, go to 74. To try to figure out a way to summon help, go to 6.

15 You continue your tour, moving on to an area filled with huge, powerful-looking mechanical devices.

'Marine engines,' states the Doctor, casting an admiring eye over one vast, gleaming hulk. 'Steam power is revolutionizing ship design, as well as running the railways.'

He leads you to a nearby stand, on which a giant steel propeller is mounted.

'Paddle-steamers came first, but now the engineers have discovered the screw propeller. They're building bigger and faster ships every year.'

Martha clutches the Doctor's arm suddenly.

'What's that?'

You, too, can hear footsteps approaching. A man in a blue top hat and brass-buttoned tailcoat is pacing among the exhibits not far from where you stand.

'Police!' hisses the Doctor.

To duck behind one of the giant engines until the police constable has passed, go to 94. To move quietly away, in the hope that he won't spot you, go to 4.

The next exhibit is a model of the Sun, Moon and Earth. Small globes representing each are supported above a wooden base — the Sun suspended from a slim boom, the others perched on thin axles.

'It's a Tellurium,' explains the Doctor. 'Represents the precise motions of the Earth and Moon through space.' He runs his sonic screwdriver around the model's casing and gingerly lifts it away to reveal an intricate mechanism of cogs and cranks.

'A hundred per cent clockwork. Beautiful, isn't it?'

He replaces the casing, then signals for you to try the winding handle. As you turn it, the miniature worlds swirl gracefully around one another.

Suddenly you hear footsteps. Someone is climbing the nearby staircase from the ground floor. The three of you quickly duck behind a display cabinet, just as a man in a long blue tailcoat, wearing a blue top hat, reaches the gallery.

'Peeler,' whispers the Doctor. 'Victorian policeman. Bound to be a few on security patrol.'

To stay hidden where you are, go to 5. To attempt to sneak further away, along the gallery, go to 24.

You beat a hasty retreat, fleeing into the central avenue — where you run headlong into the Doctor. He is standing over a small mining locomotive, from the exhibition's railway section. It is steaming gently. The Doctor is in the process of replacing its whistle with a bizarre-looking gadget that incorporates, among other things, a modified organ pipe.

'Nearly ready!' grunts the Doctor, struggling to secure the peculiar device. 'Just need a second or two to get up enough pressure.'

The creature pursuing you reaches the central avenue. Seeing the Doctor with you, it slows to a cautious approach. More creatures emerge from the other side of the nave. They spread out, surrounding you.

'It took me a little while to see the solution,' says the Doctor, tapping the pressure gauge on the locomotive's boiler impatiently. Its needle climbs, agonisingly slowly. 'I knew that for the Shryken to run billions of nanobots, their control signal would need phenomenal bandwidth. Which meant there had to be a big receiver somewhere.'

The creatures encircling you begin to close in.

'And I also knew that if I could destroy that receiver, the signal would fail, and the nanobots would cease to operate. Then it hit me — the only thing big enough to serve as the receiver is the building itself. The Crystal Palace. The Shryken use a silicon-based substance similar to glass in much of their technology. It's the vast glass surface of the Palace that's receiving the control signal.'

As the pressure gauge's needle finally twitches into the red, the Doctor looks up with a manic grin.

'So all we have to do is break the windows!'

He gives the whistle-contraption a sharp twist. A split second later, there is a cataclysmic crash as almost 300,000 panes of glass throughout the vast exhibition hall shatter simultaneously. The Doctor pulls you down under cover of the locomotive's boiler, as fragments of glass shower down from above.

With their control receiver destroyed, the Shryken nanobots are rendered inactive. All around you, the nanobotic creatures disintegrate into a lifeless mass of black granules, spilling across the wooden floor.

As the deluge and din subside, the Doctor stands, shakes the glass from his suit jacket, and gives the modified locomotive whistle a fond pat.

'High frequency resonator. Same principle as an opera singer shattering a wine glass with a high note.'

He claps his hands purposefully.

'Right — we'll give Brunel a hand freeing the people from the sampling pod, then I think we can leave him to sort out the rest of this mess. It's time Martha and I took you home. How does a trip in the TARDIS grab you?'

And putting his arm around your shoulder, he leads you away along the nave, broken glass and lifeless nanobots crunching under your feet, the vast iron-framed roof above you open to a cloudless blue sky.

THE END

The Canadian exhibits include several elegant horse-drawn sleighs, each of which is draped with samples of animal fur and whale skins. There are long, neat rows of wooden barrels, labelled WHEAT and MAPLE SUGAR. But the dominant exhibit is a huge birch-bark canoe, large enough to hold twenty men, suspended by ropes from the gallery above.

Martha gives a low whistle.

'That'd take some paddling!'

The Doctor has been admiring a horse-drawn water-pumping engine, belonging to the Canadian fire brigade. Now he signals for you to keep moving.

Without warning, a pair of nanobotic creatures come scuttling from the central avenue, hot on your trail.

To send some of the wooden barrels rolling back towards your pursuers, in order to delay them, go to 72. To clamber up into the birch-bark canoe, and climb one of the ropes suspending it, go to 26.

You hurry along the upward-sloping tunnel. After a short distance, it opens out abruptly. You find yourself on the brink of a vast underground cavern.

A massive ramp, made of smooth, colourless material, rises from the cavern floor. Clinging to its sloping surface is a squat, matt black, heart-shaped craft, around fifty metres across and slightly more in length.

'Starship,' whispers the Doctor. 'Must be how our friends got here. Certainly intergalactic — the twin vents at the back are Fission Drive exhausts.'

Nanobotic devices scuttle busily across the craft's smooth skin, like giant worker ants.

'Looks like they're getting her ready for launch.'

You are suddenly aware of a familiar gritty sound behind you. You spin to face a group of four pincer-limbed monsters as they rapidly take shape from a dark sandy pool on the tunnel floor.

To make a desperate attempt to flee, go to 55. To give yourselves up, go to 3.

Your assault has little effect — the nanobotic creatures seem all but impossible to harm. But just as it seems inevitable that they will overpower and capture you, there's an almighty crashing sound. A heavy, steel-wheeled, steam-powered tractor comes ploughing through the nearest display cabinet, driving the surprised creatures back. Brunel, grim-faced, is at the wheel.

'The boilers are up to pressure, Doctor!' he yells over the chuff-clunk of the tractor's pounding pistons. 'Get yourself to the Machinery in Motion section, and you'll have all the steam-power you need. Now GO!'

As the creatures begin to advance again, you turn and sprint away with the Doctor and Martha, leaving Brunel to keep them at bay as best he can with the steam tractor.

The Doctor quickly leads you westwards to where the transept crosses the nave at the centre of the vast glass hall. Here, you turn right. At the very northern end of the transept, a door leads into a lavishly furnished room.

'The Queen's private robing room,' pants the Doctor. 'This is where Martha and I arrived in the TARDIS.'

'The what?' you ask.

'TARDIS. My space-time ship. Big blue wooden box.' He looks around, frowning. 'But it's not here...'

He turns abruptly to you and Martha.

'Right — if it isn't here, I need to find out where it is. You two stay put — you should be safe here. I'll be back as soon as I can.'

And before Martha can reply, he's gone.

After several minutes of anxious waiting, a distant but recognisable yell reaches you from along the nave.

'That was Brunel!' says Martha. 'He's in trouble!'

And she too dashes off, in the direction of the scream.

To wait for the Doctor, go to 9. To go with Martha, go to 54.

The Australian section includes a display of hats, handmade by British convicts from the leaves of native cabbage trees.

'Australia is where Victorian Britain sends all its social outcasts,' observes Martha. 'I watched a programme about it. Orphans, misfits — but particularly convicts. Some genuinely nasty pieces of work, but quite a few unfairly charged ones, too. Some of them were just kids, accused of petty theft. Imagine being shipped to prison on the other side of the world, 10,000 miles from your friends and family.'

'Er... you may not *need* to imagine...' says the Doctor.

A police constable, responding to his fellow officer's alarm, is striding towards you.

'Doctor!' hisses Martha. 'Psychic paper!'

'Ah, yes.' The Doctor delves in his pocket and pulls out a blank piece of paper, which he thrusts under the policeman's stern gaze.

'Jeremiah Chubb of Messrs Chubb and Chubb, Locksmiths. Just checking the cabinet locks...'

To stand your ground, in the hope that the Doctor's bluff will work, go to 10. To run for it, go to 73.

The Doctor leads you a short way along the nave before halting at an octagonal pedestal. On it stands what looks like a large gilded birdcage, topped by a crown. Inside, on a velvet cushion, sits a diamond the size of an egg.

'About thirty years from now, that little beauty will save Queen Victoria's life,' states the Doctor, impressively. 'From a werewolf.'

Both you and Martha stare at him, incredulous.

'It's true!' protests the Doctor. 'Honestly! Now — let's have a closer look.'

But as the Doctor runs his sonic screwdriver around the base of the domed cage, Martha hisses a warning. A policeman is striding along the central avenue, heading in your direction.

To attempt to sneak away before the constable spots you, go to 4. To quickly find a place to hide, go to 88.

You follow Brunel as he quickly approaches a large mechanical contraption. Its overall shape reminds you of a modern-day communications satellite. A fat cylindrical drum at its centre is hugged by eight slim rollers and surrounded by a series of eight vertical screens, draped with paper.

'Applegath's vertical printing machine,' Brunel informs you, as he sets about adjusting a series of control levers. 'Installed at *The Times* just three years ago. Prints 6,000 sheets an hour.'

As he steps back, the machine grinds into life. The huge central printing cylinder begins to revolve steadily, dragging the broad sheets of paper through the slim rollers. You watch for a few moments, transfixed.

'Come on.' Brunel gestures to the neighbouring machines. 'What next — the steam hammer, or the cotton machines?'

To choose the steam hammer, go to 89.
To take a look at the cotton-making machines, go to 39.

As you edge quietly backwards, away from the patrolling policeman, Martha accidentally knocks a small glass-domed instrument from its display stand. It hits the gallery floor and smashes.

The silence that follows the crash is split by a loud *rat-a-tat-a-tat-a-tat-a-tat* sound. The police constable has spotted you, and is raising the alarm with a hand-held device he has taken from his belt. It looks rather like an old-fashioned wooden football rattle.

'They don't get whistles 'til the 1880s,' observes the Doctor, turning to run.

'Look! Another staircase!' cries Martha. The three of you quickly race down the spiralling stairwell to the ground floor, where you emerge amid a collection of gleaming horse-drawn carriages — the Victorian equivalent of a motor show.

To quickly hide inside one of the carriages, go to 38. To hurry further along the nave, go to 87.

You and Martha quickly follow Brunel along the nave. Nearing its western end, you arrive at an extensive area occupied entirely by steam-powered industrial apparatus. This is the Machinery in Motion section — though at present, the gleaming wheels and pistons are silent and still.

Brunel immediately hurries to the first of a nearby row of six large textile-weaving machines.

'Jacquard looms,' he informs you. 'For weaving wool and worsted, mostly. Usually fairly straightforward to start up.'

You watch as he demonstrates the necessary sequence of lever pulls and steam-valve turns. Sure enough, the machine comes to life, quickly settling into a rhythmic *click-clunk-whir* action.

'You start the other looms,' says Brunel. 'I'll move on to the next batch of machines.'

And he hurries away.

To help Martha start the other looms, go to 47. To go after Brunel, go to 23.

You make it to the gallery. Dashing along it – through an area displaying a collection of stained glass – you manage to put some space between yourselves and your pursuers. As the Doctor ducks behind a display cabinet, you and Martha follow suit. Moments later the nanobotic creatures scuttle past. You've escaped the danger – for now.

The Doctor is first to emerge. He crosses to the gallery rail to look out over the nave, taking stock of your whereabouts.

'The TARDIS!'

You and Martha hurry to the Doctor's side. Below, you can see a pair of giant nanobotic creatures moving slowly eastwards along the central avenue, hauling a large, dark-blue box.

'What is it?' you ask, puzzled.

'My space/time ship.'

The Doctor frowns as the creatures turn northward, and disappear from view.

'Where are they taking her? I'm going after them – you two stay here. I'll be back as soon as I can.'

And before you can protest, he dashes off.

'Look!'

This time it's Martha who has spotted something. Following her pointing finger, you see the figure of Brunel hurrying through one of the international areas below.

'Isambard!'

At Martha's shout, he looks up, gives you a friendly salute, then hollers back.

'Tell the Doctor I've got the boilers up to pressure — I'm heading for Machinery in Motion now, to see what I can get moving.'

As he turns away and continues to make his way westward, you and Martha spot a group of replicant police constables stalking him.

'He hasn't seen them!' frets Martha. 'We need to warn him…'

And she, too, hurries off purposefully.

To go with Martha, go to 54. To wait for the Doctor to return, go to 9.

You move off through an area on the north side of the nave where the produce of Prussia is displayed.

'Apparently, the Prussian king, Frederick William IV, wasn't keen on the idea of the Exhibition,' the Doctor informs you, as you hurry on. 'Thought it might make the working classes over-ambitious, and start a revolution — like the ones that tore Europe apart only a few years earlier.'

The most unusual Prussian exhibit you pass is an octagonal cast iron stove, topped with a life-size figure of a knight in plate armour, brandishing a sword.

'Certainly makes a statement,' says Martha, pulling a face. 'Can't be many people who have a knight-shaped chimney.'

The Doctor grins. But his smile vanishes as a pair of nanobotic creatures suddenly appear a little way ahead, blocking your path.

To grab the sword from the stove-top knight, and use it against the creatures, go to 20. To hurriedly retreat, go to 44.

28 The tunnel eventually leads to an underground chamber. You cautiously enter, and find yourself flanked by large transparent vats, filled to the brim with black sand. You realise — with a shiver — that this 'sand' is made up of more microscopic nanobots, in their billions.

A tall, cylindrical device stands at the centre of the chamber. Silver cables connect it to each of the vats. The Doctor inspects it silently, then delivers his verdict.

'Reactor of some kind. Feeds energy into the vats. I imagine each nanobot has a power cell — this must be where they recharge.'

A valve at the base of the nearest vat suddenly clicks open, rapidly discharging its grainy black contents. The released batch of freshly-recharged nanobots instantly begin to organise themselves. You watch, terrified, as a pair of three-metre tall cybernetic monsters take shape before your eyes.

To make a break for it, go to 55. To surrender, since capture seems inevitable, go to 3.

Descending steadily, you come to a junction with another passageway. At the sound of something approaching along it, the Doctor presses you back against the tunnel wall and puts his finger to his lips.

Seconds later, a small, many-legged nanobotic creature scuttles past along the other tunnel. It is carrying a thick crystalline slab, etched with silver lines, in its sucker-covered forelimbs.

As the creature disappears along the tunnel, the Doctor looks thoughtful.

'That looked like part of a Fission Drive, which means our nanobotic friends are building – or repairing – a starship of some kind. Which suggests they're intending to leave Earth some time soon. I wonder what they're planning to take with them…'

He breaks off at the sound of more approaching creatures. Two hulking nanobotic guards are lumbering along the intersecting tunnel.

To run for it, go to 55. To attempt to stay hidden again, go to 85.

You run for your life, heading for the central avenue. The nanobotic creatures scuttle after you, each unleashing a ball of blue light. Both projectiles fizz narrowly past.

'Stun-pulses!' yells the Doctor. 'We need to get out of the open!'

You dash for the cover of a towering stone fountain. But both creatures fire again, and this time their stun-pulses find their mark. One clips your side, before hitting the Doctor square in the back. The other strikes Martha. As you collapse, dazed, beside the fountain, your two friends slump to the floor.

The creatures rapidly dissolve into their constituent nanobots. As they recombine, once more assuming the form of a policeman, a second replicant constable arrives on the scene. Together, they begin to drag away the unconscious Martha.

You struggle to your feet, rather wobbly from the glancing stun-pulse blow, but still in one piece.

To attempt to revive the Doctor using water from the fountain, go to 80. To go after Martha, go to 48.

31 You move to the southern side of the nave, past a vast bronze-and-zinc statue of an Amazon warrior on horseback being attacked by a tiger. The statue stands at the entrance to a separate exhibition area, over which a banner reads ZOLLVEREIN.

'That's not a country, is it?' asks Martha.

'We're in the nineteenth-century, remember,' replies the Doctor. 'Europe isn't divided exactly as it will be 150 years from now. The Zollverein is a union of twenty-six separate states that'll end up becoming part of Germany. Places like Bavaria, Württemberg, Nass—'

The Doctor's political history lesson is cut short as a group of menacing-looking nanobotic creatures suddenly emerge from amid the Zollverein exhibits.

To upset a nearby stand of Bavarian beer bottles into the creatures' path, in an attempt to delay them, go to 72. To hurl individual bottles to drive them back, go to 20.

32 You follow the sound of Martha's shrieks, racing with the Doctor past one Victorian innovation after another — an envelope-making machine; a display of newly-invented safety pins; a model pneumatic railway — until you enter the international part of the nave.

You catch up with Martha's captors in the Austrian section. The replicant constables have come to a halt at the foot of a colossal four-poster zebra-wood bed — by far the largest you have ever seen.

To your amazement, the massive bed suddenly rises into the air, revealing an opening in the floor beneath. The policemen drop into the blackness of the hole, taking the struggling Martha with them.

'Who says there aren't monsters under the bed?' remarks the Doctor, darkly.

'Quick — before it closes!'

And sprinting forward, he too plunges into the blackness.

To follow the Doctor, before the bed drops back into place, go to 82. To pause for a moment, to think of a way of keeping the entrance open for your return, go to 8.

You step through the right-hand portal, to find yourself back in the nave of the Crystal Palace. A banner above your head reads SPAIN.

The Spanish exhibits range from colourful fans and beautiful mantillas — delicate lace scarves worn over the hair — to fat cigars from the Spanish colony of Cuba.

The Doctor approaches a display of swords and sabres, grasps one by its elegant hilt, and takes a few experimental swipes.

'Beautiful craftsmanship. A Toledo blade. They've been making the world's finest swords in Toledo for centuries.'

'Come on, Doctor,' urges Martha impatiently. 'Those things can't be far behind.'

Even as she speaks, several nanobotic creatures materialize from the Transmat portal, and rapidly spread out to surround you.

To grab a Toledo blade and use it to defend yourself, go to 20. To make a break for the only available escape route — the nearby stairs to the gallery — go to 26.

34 You step through the left-hand Transmat portal and find
yourself back in the Crystal Palace — at the extreme eastern
end of the nave, in the United States section.

The American exhibits range from up-to-the-minute
agricultural equipment to samples of recently discovered
Californian gold. The Doctor frowns at a nearby display of
handguns, labelled:

REVOLVING CHARGE REPEATING FIREARMS
BY SAMUEL COLT

'Colt's revolvers are one of the USA's many contributions to
weapons technology. Ten years from now another American,
Gatling, will invent the machine gun. Making it possible to
kill on a previously unimaginable scale.'

A look of deep sadness crosses the Doctor's typically
cheerful face.

'Come on — let's keep moving.'

At that moment, two nanobotic creatures burst from the
portal behind you and begin to advance menacingly.

**To grab one of the revolvers and fire it
at your approaching enemies, in the hope
of disabling them, go to 20. To run for it
along the nave, go to 44.**

As you watch, one of the replicant constables draws a stout truncheon from his tailcoat pocket. Holding it at arm's length, he gives its tip a purposeful twist. It immediately begins to emit an unearthly, ear-splitting screech.

The noise is so excruciating that you, Martha and the Doctor involuntarily stagger from your hiding place, hands clasped over your ears, desperate to get away from it.

The agonising sound stops as abruptly as it began. Having flushed you out, the constables plan to deal with you personally. As you nurse your throbbing head, they dissolve once more into a powdery black mass. The millions of tiny nanobots rapidly recombine in the form of a single cybernetic hulk.

As the Doctor bravely squares up to the monster, it spits a glowing ball of blue energy from its mouth. The projectile strikes the Doctor in the chest, sending him sprawling.

To make matters worse, two more replicant constables arrive on the scene. They knock you roughly to the floor, then grapple with Martha. Overcoming her feisty resistance, they drag her away.

To help the stricken Doctor fight the nanobotic monster, go to 36. To go after Martha, go to 46.

36 As the nanobotic creature stalks towards the Doctor, you struggle to your feet and bravely shoulder-charge the back of its legs. It topples clumsily to the floor, giving the Doctor a chance to regain his feet. The pair of you turn and flee, out into the central avenue.

The monster is soon on your tail. As it spits another energy ball, you dive for cover behind a cabinet stacked with stoppered glass bottles, each labelled:

DICKSON'S COD LIVER OIL

The Doctor grabs a bottle, and hurls it at your assailant. It smashes against the creature's artificial body, splattering it with fishy-smelling oil. You join in the bombardment. Soon oil is trickling down the creature's body to pool at its feet, causing it to slip about awkwardly.

As the creature loses its feet altogether, the Doctor whoops triumphantly. But the sound of a woman's scream — Martha's — quickly wipes the grin from his face.

To abandon the fight to go after Martha, go to 32. To continue your battle, go to 12.

You struggle from under the Doctor's unconscious body, and try desperately to revive him. After a few worrying moments, his eyelids flicker open. As he rises awkwardly to a sitting position, you quickly tell him about Martha's abduction. Moments later, he's on his feet.

'Which way did they take her?'

You sprint off together after the replicant constables. Before long you can see them up ahead. Sensing your presence, the four nanobotic policemen halt, turn, and begin to mutate once more. Within seconds, their constituent nanobots have reorganised themselves to form a pair of large, multi-headed creatures. Their numerous mouths spit a barrage of stun-pulses in your direction.

With the Doctor's sonic shield exhausted, you know it is perilous to attack — a single pulse strike could render you senseless. But there's Martha to think of…

To charge fearlessly at the creatures, attempting to dodge the stun-pulses, go to 14. To hang back, then follow them as they withdraw, go to 92.

When the danger has passed, you emerge quietly from your hiding place.

'Let's try the south side,' says the Doctor.

He leads you cautiously across the nave's central avenue. It stretches away as far as the eye can see under its breathtaking glass roof, packed with an amazing variety of exhibits. Some are enormous: a giant nineteenth-century lighthouse reflector mechanism; a magnificent astronomical telescope; a towering multi-tiered fountain.

Above you, flagpoles extend from the balconies on either side.

'The flags show the coats of arms of British towns and cities,' explains the Doctor. 'Further along, in the east nave, you've got the national flags of each exhibiting country.'

He gestures to the nearest display areas on the south side of the nave.

'Now — whaddya fancy — Hardware or Agricultural Implements?'

To explore the Hardware section, go to 40.
To look around the Agricultural exhibits, go to 7.

The cotton-making line includes over a dozen massive machines, and occupies a large area, bordered by a safety railing. Ducking under it, Brunel leads you to a group of barrel-shaped devices. He lifts the cover of one, revealing a spiked drum within.

'These are carding machines. They comb the fibres of the raw cotton, before it moves on to the slubbing frames, roving frames and spinners.'

You watch closely as he operates the necessary controls to set the first cotton-carder in motion. As it hisses into life, he turns back to you.

'Do you think you can manage the others? I'll deal with the steam hammer.'

And he hurries away.

You've just succeeded in getting a second carding machine running, when something drops from the drive belts overhead and hits the floor beside the first machine — a large, grotesque nanobotic creature.

To attempt to shove the creature backwards onto the spiked drum of the carding machine, go to 42. To run for it, go to 17.

40 As you browse the delights of the Hardware section — including a penknife with eighty blades — the Doctor stops at a display of locks. He picks one up, and beckons to you and Martha.

'I've heard about this little beauty. The Chubb Detector Lock. Back in 1832, the Chubb brothers set a challenge that nobody could pick it. In nearly twenty years, nobody's managed to. Apparently, somebody cracks it for the first time here, at the Great Exhibition.'

The Doctor pulls out his sonic screwdriver, and momentarily touches it to the lock's keyhole. There's a barely audible click.

'Well, whaddya know?' he beams. 'It's me!'

A heavy footfall behind you wipes the smile from his face. You turn to confront a stern-faced police constable.

'Ah, good morning officer,' blurts the Doctor, hastily withdrawing a piece of paper from his pocket, and holding it up. 'The Right Honourable Thomas Croddle, one of Her Majesty's Commissioners…'

To stand your ground, and hope that the Doctor's bluff somehow comes off, go to 10. To run for it, go to 73.

Further along the gallery, you come to an impressive collection of Victorian timekeeping devices, from elegant pocket watches to large ornamental clocks. One giant clock includes a moving panorama of day and night, a miniature church with working belfry and bell-ringers, and a mechanical bird organ.

'Blimey!' exclaims Martha, reading the exhibit's plaque. 'It says here that it took Mr Jacob Loudan thirty-four years to make this!'

The Doctor huffs indignantly. 'Don't get me wrong, I think time's very important — heck, I'm a Time Lord — but that seems a little excessive.'

Suddenly you spot an imposing figure approaching from along the gallery. He is a tall Victorian gentleman in tailcoat and top hat, both of which are dark blue. He appears not to have noticed you yet.

'A Peeler!' whispers the Doctor. 'A Metropolitan Police officer. Come on…'

To move stealthily along the gallery, away from the police constable, go to 51. To quickly take the nearby stairs down from the gallery, go to 58.

Your plan works perfectly — as the nanobotic creature becomes entangled in the machine's powerful steam-driven mechanism, its cybernetic body is pulverised, smashed into tiny black granules.

But wherever these granules land, they immediately begin to coalesce, coming together to form several distinct pools. A new creature rises from each, smaller than the original, but no less deadly.

You sprint away, out into the nave's central avenue. To your great relief, Martha and Brunel are there, too. But they are staring blankly ahead, terror-struck. You follow their gaze, and see why.

Several hundred nanobotic creatures are advancing menacingly along the nave. The newly-formed creatures that were pursuing you scuttle to join them. You sense that you are now facing the entire nanobotic host, come to make a final reckoning.

'Gangway! Cavalry coming through!'

You turn to see the Doctor hurrying towards you from the other end of the nave. He is wheeling what looks like a headless metal horse ahead of him. As he draws nearer, you can see that it is actually a steam boiler, mounted on four legs on a wheeled base. It has several long, thin protrusions, and a most un-Victorian-looking bundle of electronics strapped to its left flank.

As he approaches, there is a familiar rasping sound behind you. The nanobots are recombining once more. The entire host of creatures dissolve into one huge pool, from which rises a single massive, twenty-metre-tall cybernetic Goliath.

You cower at the foot of the gigantic monster, awestruck. But the Doctor remains unfazed. Reaching for a small button on the boiler device's electronic patch, he smiles up at his colossal adversary.

'Very impressive. Now *I've* got a shock for you.'

As he presses the button, a crackling bolt of energy leaps from the boiler's largest protrusion to strike the towering monster. Its vast cybernetic body instantly crumbles, dissolving into its constituent nanobots. And this time, as they shower to the floor in their billions, they lay still.

As the last nanobot hits the deck, and silence falls, the Doctor regards the four-legged steam boiler affectionately.

'Who says steam power's outdated, eh? This is a cracking little device — a "hydro-electric machine" the Victorians call it. Turns steam power into static electricity. Just needed a few modifications to crank the charge up by a factor of a thousand or so, and you have yourself a very effective voltage surge generator. Fried the nanobots' tiny processors to a crisp.'

He picks up a handful of nanobots and lets them trickle through his fingers.

'The Shryken won't be abducting anybody with these any time soon.'

'So!' he continues purposefully. 'We'd best get down to that Shryken pod and free those poor people. And then, my young friend, a trip in the TARDIS beckons. It's time Martha and I took you home.'

And together the four of you head for the nearest Transmat portal, lifeless nanobots crunching satisfyingly under your feet.

THE END

43 As you bravely confront the advancing constables, the first one produces a stout truncheon and aims it at the Doctor. An energy pulse — like the ones the nanobotic creatures have been spitting at you — shoots from its tip.

The Doctor's shield once again absorbs the energy of the stun-pulse. But as it does so, it begins to glow and crackle.

'It's rupturing!' yells the Doctor. 'It won't take ano—'

He is cut off as a pulse from the second constable's truncheon sends him sprawling backwards into you. You both hit the floor, the Doctor unconscious, you temporarily trapped beneath him.

By now, the nanobotic creatures dragging Martha away are some way off. You watch as they recombine as a single replicant policeman. The other three constables join them, and the group moves off, taking Martha with them.

To follow Martha, go to 48. To attempt to revive the Doctor, go to 37.

You run for your life along the central avenue, past a giant gothic-style church organ and numerous statues. One particular exhibit — a large blue box with POLICE PUBLIC CALL BOX written across its top — strikes you as strangely out of place. They didn't have telephones in the 1850s, did they?

The Doctor dashes up to the blue box, opens one of its narrow double doors, and ducks inside, with Martha close behind him. Puzzled, you follow.

What you find inside is mind-blowing. Somehow, despite its modest exterior dimensions, the box's interior is vast — a cavernous space with a raised central platform, where the Doctor is now bent over some sort of control console, frantically operating its levers and buttons.

Martha notices your dumbfounded expression, and grins.

'Mad, isn't it?' She pulls the door closed behind you, as you continue to stare open-mouthed.

'It's called the TARDIS. It's the Doctor's ship — how he travels between different times and dimensions.'

The Doctor gives a final control button a hearty slap, then straightens up, smiling.

'There — that should do it. I've shut down any systems that might draw our nanobotic friends' attention. They should scuttle on past like we're just another exhibit. Now — let's see what we've got lying about...'

And he begins rifling through the scattered techno-junk, occasionally muttering an 'Aha!' before stuffing a particular item in one of his suit pockets. After a few minutes, he seems satisfied.

'I'll need a few bits and bobs from the exhibition, too, to put together something effective. We'd best get back out there.'

He leads you and Martha back outside the TARDIS door — where you collide with Brunel. Like you, he has been puzzling over the strange blue box.

'Doctor — I've got the boilers up to pressure.'

'Fantastic!' replies the Doctor. 'You and Martha head for the Machinery in Motion section and see what you can get running. That should divert the nanobots' attention, while I see what I can come up with.'

And he dashes off.

To go with the Doctor, go to 49. To go with Martha and Brunel, go to 25.

To your great surprise, first one of the cotton machines, then another, and then another, slowly begin to move. Soon the entire group is clanking and chuffing noisily. As the overhead wheels and drive-belts whir into life, the creatures clambering among them are pulverised — ground into black powder, which trickles to the floor below.

Martha lets out a whoop of delight.

'Got 'em!'

But your triumph is short-lived. The powder immediately begins to form several distinct pools. The creatures' constituent nanobots are recombining again. Only moments after the creatures seemed destroyed, they are rising once more from the black pools all around.

Martha rests her hands on your shoulders and looks you in the eyes.

'I'll keep them busy — you run like the wind, OK?'

But as you do as she asks, one of the newly-formed creatures breaks off to follow you.

To keep running, go to 17. To stand and fight the creature, go to 63.

46 | Following Martha's shrieks, you pick up the replicant constables' trail. You pursue them along the nave, to a point where a high-roofed transept crosses it. Here, they turn north. A little way ahead, spanning the transept, stands a magnificent set of wrought iron gates.

Martha's nanobotic captors run straight at the iron railings of the closed gates — and vanish into thin air.

Rapid footfalls sound behind you. It's the Doctor, seemingly recovered.

'The Coalbrookdale Gates,' he pants, hurrying forward to scan his sonic screwdriver across the elaborate railings. 'Still around in your day — between Hyde Park and Kensington Gardens. Our friends appear to have converted them into a Transmat portal.'

The tip of the sonic screwdriver suddenly flares brightly.

'Ah-ha! Got it!'

He turns to give you a firm look.

'Wait here.'

And he strides into the gates, and vanishes.

To wait for the Doctor's return, go to 70. To disregard his instructions, and follow him through the Transmat portal, go to 86.

You and Martha soon have the next loom running smoothly. You're working on the third, when the Doctor suddenly appears.

'Martha — do you remember that little gadget we saw just after we arrived? *Pike's Magneto-Electrical Machine.* I need a component from it, but I can't for the life of me recollect where it was.'

'No problem, Doctor. I remember. I'll fetch it. Meet you back here in five minutes.'

As Martha hurries away, the Doctor regards the Jacquard looms with interest.

'Believe it or not, these are the direct forerunners of the computer. The first programmable devices — they use machine-read punch-cards to set the patterns.' He claps his hands. 'Right — best track down the other stuff I need...'

And he too rushes off.

You set about starting the remaining looms single-handedly. Just as you get the final one clattering into motion, a nanobotic creature stalks into sight, drawn by the noise. It hasn't seen you yet.

To hurry after the Doctor, go to 49. To attempt to lure the creature into the workings of one of the looms, go to 42.

48 You hurry after the replicant policemen as they drag Martha to where the long east-west nave is crossed by a shorter north-south transept. Two giant elm trees stand within the transept, which has a breathtaking arched glass roof to accommodate them.

The constables halt below the ancient elms. You watch as one of them traces a diamond-shape in thin air. Green light suddenly spills through it, as though through a window. To your amazement, the constables, dragging Martha with them, step through the glowing window, and vanish. An instant later, the diamond disappears.

'Transmat portal.'

You jump at the sound of the Doctor's voice. He has caught up with you, revived, if still a little dazed-looking.

He hurries forward to trace an identical diamond outline with his sonic screwdriver. The window in the air appears once more. As the Doctor steps through it, you're right behind him.

You find yourselves in a wide underground tunnel. It is lit by the eerie glow of fluorescent green ribs that reinforce the rock walls. There's no sign of Martha or her captors.

To follow the tunnel to your left, go to 28.
To go right, go to 53.

You accompany the Doctor on his hunt for components. The search takes you past a display of early photographic images — monotone portraits of public figures, family groups, and famous places.

'Daguerreotypes,' states the Doctor. 'The first proper photographs, invented by a French chemist called Louis Daguerre. It's an ingenious process — uses a silver-coated copper plate. But pretty deadly, too — the Mercury vapour used to develop the image is highly toxic.'

He rummages through the photographic equipment displayed alongside the daguerreotypes, muttering to himself.

'A lens... excellent... and another... now, if I can get hold of a semi-conductor from the Minerals section...'

He abandons his search and turns back to you.

'Back in two ticks — wait here!'

And he strides away purposefully.

Minutes pass, with no sign of the Doctor's return. You decide to take a look at the neighbouring exhibits while you're waiting.

To explore the exhibits to your left, go to 11.
To browse those on your right, go to 69.

You hurry through the area where produce from the Bahamas and Trinidad — both British colonies — is on display. Among the exhibits are barrels of whale oil, dried vanilla pods, vases made from delicate white shells, and a variety of foodstuffs in sacks.

'Muscovado sugar and cocoa beans,' observes the Doctor. 'Harvested on the plantations of Trinidad. At least they're no longer worked by slaves — slavery was abolished throughout the Empire in 1833.'

'It must be heavy-going in such a hot climate,' says Martha. 'And the beans are for making chocolate, aren't they? Another reason I ought to give it up.'

Without warning, a dozen dog-sized, tarantula-like nanobotic creatures come scurrying rapidly down several of the iron columns that support the gallery above. Reaching the floor, they immediately begin to close in.

To run for it, go to 44. To hinder the creatures' pursuit by spilling cocoa beans over the floor, go to 72.

The Silks and Satins section of the gallery boasts a rich variety of nineteenth-century textiles. As well as rail upon rail draped with the finest silk, there is a range of high-quality Victorian hosiery, an assortment of fashionable ladies' shawls, and a collection of tartans.

'Oo, some of this stuff is *gorgeous*!' enthuses Martha. 'Do you think there's a Jones family tartan?'

'Before the Industrial Revolution, this lot would all have been handmade,' observes the Doctor. 'Now they've got mechanical looms churning it out.'

Martha drapes a silk shawl around her shoulders.

'Yes, very lovely,' says the Doctor impatiently. 'But the power-looms and silk-mills themselves are more my cup of tea. Come on — they're downstairs in the Machinery in Motion section.'

He heads for the nearby staircase.

To follow the Doctor, go to 90. To take a better look at the textiles, with Martha, go to 66.

The Doctor's trusty sonic screwdriver doesn't let you down. As it deactivates the locking system, the cell's door hisses open. You step out into the chamber cautiously. There's no sign of your enemies.

'Help me! Please!'

The cry — a man's — comes from beside the transparent sampling pod. You can see a figure strapped to a silver slab. The Doctor hurries to free him.

As you help him into a sitting position, the man smiles his thanks. He is middle-aged and smartly-dressed.

'They were preparing me for a capsule, like the others,' he explains. 'My name's Brunel. Isambard Kingdom Brunel.'

'The renowned Victorian engineer!' The Doctor shakes Brunel's hand warmly. 'Pleasure to meet you. I'm the Doctor, and thi—'

His introductions are cut short, as a pair of nanobotic creatures suddenly scuttle through the chamber's doorway.

'Quick!' urges the Doctor. 'The Transmat portal!' He rushes to the far side of the chamber, where a diamond-shaped window of absolute blackness hovers in mid-air. Diving through it, he vanishes.

You, Martha and Brunel quickly follow, and find yourselves

instantly transported back to the nave of the Crystal Palace. As the Doctor hurriedly traces around the border of the portal with his sonic screwdriver, it blinks out of life.

'That's sealed — for now, at least.'

He turns to Brunel.

'If we're going to fight these nanobots, we need some form of power. Any ideas?'

'The steam-powered machinery in the west nave is supplied by a system of under-floor pipes from the main boiler room,' replies Brunel. 'If I can reach that, I should be able to get pressure up to run the machines.'

At a nod from the Doctor, he hurries away.

'We'd better make ourselves scarce, too,' says the Doctor. 'That portal won't hold for ever.'

To head into the northern side of the exhibition, go to 27. To move off through the southern side, go to 31.

53 After a short distance, the tunnel leads to an entrance. You peer cautiously into the circular chamber beyond. A large silver sphere stands at its centre. A dozen small nanobotic worker-creatures are busily clearing rock fragments from the floor, methodically vaporising each one in turn.

The Doctor silently slips out his sonic screwdriver and points it at the sphere. After a few seconds, he whispers to you.

'It's some sort of generator — I'd guess it's powering the nanobots somehow. The readings certainly aren't terrestrial.'

As he aims the sonic screwdriver once more, the sphere suddenly lets out a shrill, ear-splitting alarm.

Alerted to your presence, the squad of rubble-clearers instantly dissolve into their constituent nanobots. These rapidly recombine to form a pair of large, vicious-looking monstrosities.

To surrender, before the nanobotic creatures move in for the kill, go to 3. To hurl some of the rock fragments, in an attempt to drive them back, go to 85.

54 | You hurry after Martha, and soon find yourself passing an array of massive steam-powered machines, grouped together within a railed-off enclosure. There are fifteen in total, of varied design, clearly organised so as to form a production line. A plaque mounted on the safety railing reads:

HIBBERT, PLATT & SONS, COTTON MANUFACTURERS

As you pass the impressive machines, you look up at the vast overhead drive-wheels and belts that convey power from one to the next — and your heart sinks. Clambering down from the gallery via the machinery's overhead workings are a pair of monstrous nanobotic creatures.

Martha has seen them, too. She pulls up at what appears to be the main controls for the cotton manufacturing line, and begins frantically yanking levers and releasing steam-cocks.

To help Martha get the cotton-making machinery running, go to 45. To split up and run for it, go to 2.

As you flee in one direction, the Doctor heads in the other, bravely attempting to draw the creatures away. Alone, you sprint along the green-lit tunnel until it suddenly opens into a cavernous chamber.

A large, transparent, cylindrical pod, the size of a London Tube carriage, stands at the centre of the chamber. Inside it you can see fifty or so people, each enclosed within an individual gel-filled capsule.

'Over here!'

Martha is calling to you from the far side of the chamber. She is pinned inside a silver booth by wrist and ankle restraints. As you hurry to help her, she manages a strained smile.

'Do you think you can free us, child?'

The question comes not from Martha, but from a stranger held within a second booth alongside hers. He is a middle-aged, well-dressed Victorian gentleman. Martha introduces you.

'This is Mr Brunel. Isambard Kingdom Brunel — the famous engineer. He got nabbed by those nanobotic things, too.' She nods towards the transparent pod. 'Looks like we're not the only ones…'

To attempt to prise open the restraints holding Martha and Brunel, go to 74. To try to figure out how to release them using the booths' control panels, go to 6.

56 You and Martha anxiously accompany the Doctor as he emerges from hiding and boldly approaches the pair of replicant policemen. But before he can even speak, the first constable raises his truncheon and unleashes a pulse of fizzing blue energy directly at him.

The Doctor nimbly dodges the energy pulse. Whipping out his sonic screwdriver, he thrusts it at the attacking policeman's shoulder. As the constable's entire arm falls to the floor, the Doctor holds up the sonic screwdriver with a grin.

'Great for negating nanobotic bonds!'

But his smile quickly fades. The severed arm is dissolving into a mass of black powder. Within seconds, its constituent nanobots have recombined as a crab-like creature. Its lethal foreclaws crackle with blue energy.

As the creature launches itself at the Doctor, the constables advance on Martha, and attempt to drag her away. You try to fight them off, but are sent reeling by a bruising blow.

By the time you pick yourself up, the constables are out of sight, and Martha's screams are fast receding. You stagger over to assist the Doctor — just as the nanobotic creature fighting him suddenly turns and scuttles away.

'Rats!' curses the Doctor. 'If we could capture that little monster, we'd have a better idea what we're dealing with.'

To pursue the creature, go to 81. To follow Martha's screams, go to 32.

The stairs descend to the ground floor of the vast glass palace. They take you to an area where an impressive fleet of up-to-the-minute Victorian steam locomotives proudly stand.

'Aha — the Age of Steam!' enthuses the Doctor. He strolls between the iron giants, lovingly stroking their gleaming boilers. Alongside examples of the latest 'express' locomotives are replicas of some of their most famous forerunners — *Puffing Billy*, the first commercial steam locomotive, and George Stephenson's celebrated *Rocket*.

'Only twenty years since they opened the first line,' observes the Doctor. 'And now there's over 6000 miles of track, connecting nearly every major town in England.'

Martha is eyeing an open-sided carriage with basic wooden seats. 'Doesn't look very comfy, though,' she comments.

'Don't knock it,' replies the Doctor. 'Until a few years ago, third class carriages didn't have seats at all. Or a roof.'

To continue west along the nave, go to 76.
To head east, go to 15.

Your escape route doesn't work out quite as planned — there is another top-hatted police constable patrolling the area at the foot of the stairs. The Doctor leads you silently back up to the gallery. You creep along it, away from the original policeman, who is still pacing the Philosophical Instruments section.

Just as you appear to have made your getaway, you spot a *third* constable moving towards you from the opposite end of the gallery.

'What now?' Martha hisses anxiously. 'We're trapped!'

The Doctor desperately scans the area. 'Well, we either hide somehow, 'til they've gone, or...' He peers over the gallery railings to the ground floor several metres below. Directly beneath you is the fabric canopy of an enormous four-poster bed.

'Or we *could* take the plunge!'

To brave the jump down, go to 79. To conceal yourself behind one of the display cabinets, go to 5.

Your attempt to go unnoticed is in vain. The police constable levels a cold stare at you, and strides in your direction.

'Not to worry!' says the Doctor, flamboyantly pulling a sheet of blank paper from his pocket, as though it represents the solution to your predicament. 'Psychic paper,' he confides in you, with a wink.

You gaze blankly at him.

'To PC Plod here, it'll look like whatever official document we need to authorise our presence,' explains Martha. 'Watch.'

But what happens next takes even the Doctor by surprise. Having approached to within a few metres, the police constable comes to a halt. He stands perfectly still, as if frozen. Then, to your astonishment, the entire surface of his body begins to shift and slide downwards, its colour darkening as it does so. It is as though he is slipping away in layers, dissolving into a flowing mass of opaque black that quickly pools on the wooden floor. Despite its fluid movement, there is no wetness to this pool — the gritty, rasping sound that accompanies its motion suggests that it is made up of tiny hard granules, like coarse black sand.

'Nanobots,' hisses the Doctor, his brow furrowing. 'Millions of them. Miniature robotic units that can assemble themselves into an infinite variety of functional combinations — in this case a replica human. Shape-shifting robots, if you like. *Very* advanced technology.'

As the constable's lower body spills on to the floor, the black pool separates into two. From the surface of each smaller pool, a new form begins to rise. It is like watching something melt, in reverse. As the pools rapidly diminish, two altogether new entities take shape in the place of the policeman — multi-limbed spider-like creatures, each the size of a large dog. Once complete, they scuttle menacingly towards you.

To stand your ground, go to 78. To run for it, go to 30.

60 You sprint up the staircase to the gallery above and hurry along it to the east, looking out over the main exhibition area below in the hope of catching sight of Martha.

Sure enough, you spot her, not far off, being dragged along the nave by her nanobotic captors.

There is a staircase back down from the gallery just up ahead. You hurriedly make for it — only to see another replicant constable ascending the stairs, blocking your way.

Retracing your steps to the original staircase will take valuable time — you're likely to lose track of Martha. You look over the gallery railings at the ground floor several metres below. There's a definite chance you could make the jump unhurt. But it's a long drop. Fall awkwardly, and you'll knock yourself out cold.

To dodge past the constable down the staircase ahead, go to 48. To hang from the gallery, then let go, go to 14.

As you pray that your enemy won't discover you, a shrill whistling sound suddenly fills the air. Peering out from your hiding place, you are surprised to see the creature twitching awkwardly, as though affected by the continuing whistling. It turns, and moves off falteringly in the direction of the noise.

Intrigued by what is drawing the creature away, you follow. As it makes its way along the nave's central avenue, more creatures emerge to join it, all moving clumsily. It seems the entire host of nanobots is being drawn towards the sound, like rats to the Pied Piper's flute.

The creatures — in their hundreds now — rapidly converge on the very centre of the Palace, where the nave and transept cross. Here, the exhibition's central ornament — the breathtaking Crystal Fountain — proudly stands. It is over eight metres tall, with three umbrella-like tiers of finely cut and polished glass, rising to a slim, sparkling jet at its apex.

Clinging with one hand to the fountain's very top is the Doctor. His sonic screwdriver, clutched in his other hand, is emitting the high-pitched sound. As the horde of nanobotic creatures encircle the fountain, he slips it into his pocket, and takes out a second gadget. In the silence that has now fallen, he addresses the monstrous assembly.

'I thought that would get your attention! If I calculated the frequency correctly, that will have played havoc with your inter-cell communication — must have been extremely annoying. Anyhow, now you're all here, I'd like to show you something.'

He holds up the odd device.

'My very own proton accelerator, made entirely from nineteenth-century bits and pieces. Rather proud of it. Doesn't look much — but watch this!'

He touches the device to the top of the Crystal Fountain. A bolt of red energy shoots down the fountain's glass stem. As it strikes the cut-glass prisms of the bottom tier, the beam is split and angled. A 360-degree horizontal fan of energy explodes from the fountain in an expanding ring, striking every one of the surrounding nanobotic creatures. As it does so, they disintegrate.

As the last creature crumbles into its component nanobots, silence falls. The Doctor pockets the device, and begins to clamber down the fountain. You hurry forward to join him. Together, you survey the powdery black mass lying lifeless all around.

'Amazing how much damage a proton beam can do,' says the Doctor. 'Burnt out their nanoprocessors. They'll not cause any more trouble.'

He turns to you.

'Which means that while Brunel gets a dustpan and brush, you, me and Martha can go and free those people in the sampling pod. After that, we'd better find the TARDIS, and get you back where you belong. Before anybody notices you're missing and calls the police.'

He flashes you a grin.

'We've had enough trouble with them for one day.'

THE END

As you head for the African section, the Doctor halts abruptly.

'Hang on! I nearly forgot one of my favourites!'

He leads you a little further along the nave to where a headless metal mannequin stands at the centre of a roped-off circle.

'Count Dunin's "Man of Steel",' announces the Doctor. 'I'm not a fan of mechanical men in general,' — he flashes Martha a knowing look — 'but this one's rather delightful. He's got over 7,000 pieces. His outer surface is made from slips of steel and copper, and when you turn his winding handle, the internal mechanism makes them expand. He can change from a little five-foot chap to a big burly six-foot-eight fella. Truly ingeni—'

He breaks off, signalling urgently for you and Martha to duck down. A second policeman, responding to his fellow constable's alarm, is hurrying along the nave.

To quickly find a hiding place, go to 88.
To keep still and silent, in the hope that the constable will pass without noticing you, go to 59.

You bravely confront the nanobotic monster, certain that death is only moments away.

But as the creature advances menacingly, something odd begins to happen. One of its several limbs suddenly begins to twitch, then thrash around violently. As a second leg starts flaying about wildly, the creature staggers to a standstill, unable to coordinate its movement.

The Doctor steps into view a little way off. In one hand he is carrying a peculiar antenna-like device — the frame of an umbrella lashed to a brass-tipped shooting stick. In his other hand, attached to the antenna by a wire, is something you recognise from history lessons — a simple telegraph transmitter.

As the Doctor approaches, you can see that he is tapping away frantically on the transmitter. As he does so, the creature's cybernetic body is wracked with more convulsions. One of its limbs comes away completely, falling to the floor.

Beyond the Doctor, you see many more creatures emerging from among the exhibits. The entire nanobotic host appears to be converging on the Doctor, desperate to stop what he is doing. But as they approach, each one begins to behave like the first, jerking and jolting erratically, shedding body fragments.

'I've found the transmission frequency of the Shryken's control signal!' yells the Doctor to you, tapping away furiously. 'If I keep disrupting the signal with interference from this transmitter, I should be able to make the nanobots terminally malfunction — permanently crash their systems.'

Sure enough, the creature nearest to you gives one final heaving convulsion, then disintegrates altogether. Its constituent nanobots sprinkle to the floor, then fall still. One after another, the entire host of nanobotic creatures follow suit, silently crumbling into black granular heaps.

Martha and Brunel burst on to the scene, pulling up in amazement at the sight of the deactivated nanobots. The Doctor, still clasping his bizarre transmitter, gives them a wide grin. Then he turns to speak to you.

'Right. We'd best get back down to the Shryken pod and rescue those poor people inside. Then, my friend, it's time Martha and I gave you a TARDIS ride home.'

You nod. But before you move off, you ask the Doctor what telegraphic message he had used to such devastating effect.

'I just kept repeating the same signal,' smiles the Doctor. 'Dot-dot-dot, dash-dash-dash, dot-dot-dot. Morse Code for the letters SOS — *Save Our Souls*.'

He surveys the powdery mass of lifeless nanobots strewn across the hall's wooden floor.

'And it did, didn't it?'

THE END

You manage, at last, to shift the stubborn valve. But despite your best efforts, you still cannot coax the crushing-mill into life. Whichever controls you try, it refuses to respond.

Then, suddenly, Brunel is at your side.

'Hold back this lever until the needle on the pressure gauge reaches the green,' he instructs you, guiding your hand on to a smooth brass handle. 'Then release it, and the conveyor and crusher should start running nicely.'

As he hurries off to fire up some of the other machines, you watch the rising pressure dial as instructed. Then, out of the corner of your eye, you notice a nearby movement. A nanobotic creature is patrolling the area to the far side of the crushing-mill. It hasn't spotted you yet.

As your pulse quickens, the needle on the pressure gauge reaches the green.

To lure the creature towards you, on to the crushing-mill's conveyor belt, then release the lever, go to 42. To hurry away after Brunel, go to 23.

The Doctor stoops to pick up the stricken nanobotic creature. As he touches it, its surface suddenly flares with blue light. He gives a yell of pain and reels backwards, staggering drunkenly.

'Aarghh... idiot!' the Doctor reprimands himself. 'It's got... ahh... a residual... stun field. Could've... nurrghh... knocked me out...'

He gives his head a vigorous shake, then approaches the immobilised creature once more, taking out his sonic screwdriver.

'Should be able to disable it,' he mutters, poking gingerly around the creature's underbelly. 'If I bypass this...'

A moment later, his concentration is broken by a woman's shriek.

'Martha!'

The Doctor is on his feet in an instant. Abandoning the nanobotic device, he dashes off in the direction of Martha's scream.

To follow the Doctor, go to 32. To take a look at the disabled creature yourself, assuming the Doctor has now deactivated its stun field, go to 14.

You look through a selection of the Victorian fabrics and garments with Martha, until she gestures towards the staircase.

'We'd better get after him. He'll only get in trouble otherwise.'

You follow her downstairs to an area full of nineteenth-century agricultural equipment. Basic ploughs, hoes and rakes share the space with more complicated mechanical implements, some steam-powered.

The Doctor is cheerfully browsing a collection of beehives. Alongside the standard hive are a number of custom-designed ones, including a replica of a Victorian town house.

'Look! A little house for bees! Do you think it has a tiny throne for the queen?'

The Doctor's smile slips momentarily as a policeman steps from behind a nearby display cabinet, truncheon in hand.

'Ahh. Constable.' The Doctor hastily produces a seemingly blank piece of paper from his pocket. He holds it up, beaming. 'Thomas Bazley esquire, Exhibition Commisioner — just doing the rounds!'

To stand your ground in the hope that the Doctor's bluff works, go to 10. To run for it, go to 73.

You step through the left-hand Transmat portal and find yourself back in the Crystal Palace. You are standing amid an impressive display of ornate vases, expertly crafted in porcelain and glass.

'From the nineteenth-century glass capital – Vienna,' says the Doctor. 'We must have come out in the Austrian section.'

Just ahead is the entrance to an area dedicated to Austrian sculpture. It is bordered by heavy satin drapes, hung from the gallery above.

'Come on,' urges the Doctor. 'It can't be long before our nanobotic friends discover our cell is empty.'

Even as he speaks, a pair of fearsome robotic creatures burst from the portal behind you.

To quickly climb the thick drapes to escape to the gallery, go to 26. To run for it, go to 44.

Bottles and phials line the cabinets here. Martha is browsing the nineteenth-century cures with fascination. The Doctor, joining you, plucks a bottle from a shelf, and raises an eyebrow.

'Now here's a drop of medical history.'

Removing the stopper, he holds the bottle towards you.

'Have a sniff — but very gently.'

The liquid's vapour is slightly sweet. Inhaling it makes you feel woozy.

'Chloroform — one of the earliest anaesthetics. First used in 1847. Until this came along, all you got to see you through an operation was a stiff drink.'

He re-stoppers the bottle and replaces it.

'If it's medical history you want, Martha, they've got surgical instruments downstairs. Come on!'

The nearby staircase takes the three of you down to the ground floor. But as you reach it, another police constable strides into view, patrolling the displays only metres away.

To keep very still and silent, in the hope that the constable will pass without noticing you, go to 59. To attempt to hide, go to 88.

69 The adjacent area is packed with anatomical models of all shapes and sizes. A plaque informs you that they are the creations of Doctor Louis Auzoux, a Parisian inventor, who has skilfully crafted them from papier-maché.

The models are designed to be taken apart to reveal their subject's anatomical structure. They claim to represent 'the organization of all species of beings' — from a half-size model of a horse, to a giant silkworm nearly a metre long. Most, though, illustrate human anatomy. There is a giant eye, a multi-piece brain, and a series of models depicting the growth of a human foetus.

You are enjoying taking apart a 130-piece life-size human body when you hear a noise. A nanobotic creature is prowling nearby. Your instinct is to yell for the Doctor, but this will only draw the creature's attention — it hasn't seen you yet.

To try to hide before the creature spots you, go to 61. To prepare to defend yourself by hurling papier-maché body parts at it, go to 63.

You watch the gates for a few moments, keenly awaiting the Doctor's return. Then, with a sinking feeling, you sense something behind you. Turning, you see four replicant constables closing in, in a semicircle. Without hesitation, you turn back, and stride forward into the gates.

Passing through the Transmat portal gives you a momentary sickly sensation. You find yourself in totally new surroundings — midway along an underground tunnel. It is eerily lit by the glow of strange fluorescent ribs that reinforce the circular rock walls.

The Doctor is a few metres further along the tunnel. As you hurry to join him, you hear a double thud behind you. The nanobotic constables have followed you through the portal — but only after recombining to form a pair of huge, deadly-looking cyber-creatures.

To surrender to the creatures, go to 3.
To attempt to fight them off, go to 85.

After several minutes of trying, to no avail, you give up. The situation seems hopeless. Then, unexpectedly, the door of the cell hisses open. Standing outside is a very bedraggled-looking middle-aged Victorian gentleman.

'To whom do we owe our freedom?' beams the Doctor, as you step out gratefully.

'Brunel,' replies the man.

The Doctor looks intrigued.

'As in Isambard Kingdom Brunel, the famous engineer?'

'The same. I was taken by the police-creatures, like you. But I managed to escape. I've been hiding out in their godforsaken tunnels for the last two days.'

'Then let's see if we can get you out of here.'

Sonic screwdriver in hand, the Doctor leads you swiftly from the chamber, along a deserted tunnel, until you reach a spot where three diamond-shaped windows of pitch blackness hover impossibly before you.

'Transmat portals,' says the Doctor, hurriedly scanning the central one. 'According to these readings, this one should open onto the north side of the west nave.'

He turns to Brunel.

'That's where the boiler house that generates the steam for the machine exhibits is, isn't it? If you can fire up the boilers, we might be able to use some of the machines to tackle the creatures — or at least distract them.'

Brunel nods resolutely. Without further ado, he steps through the central portal, and vanishes.

'We'd better try one of the others,' says the Doctor. 'And see what we can dig up to surprise our nanobotic friends.'

To take the left-hand portal, go to 67. To take the right-hand one, go to 84.

Your quick-thinking pays off — as the creatures struggle to negotiate the hazard, you seize your chance to make a swift getaway.

You and Martha are hurrying along the nave after the Doctor, when he comes to an abrupt halt at the foot of a colossal zinc statue of Queen Victoria.

'Hang on — I recognise this,' mutters the Doctor. 'If we head over here…'

He turns sharply to his right and strides purposefully into an area displaying French furniture. After a few paces, he suddenly ducks down, signalling urgently for you to do the same. A little way ahead, a dozen replicant police constables are gathered around a particular object. To your eyes, it looks like just another exhibit — an antique police phone box. Then it dawns on you — in 1851, the phone hadn't been invented. Weird.

'It's the TARDIS,' Martha whispers to you, as though reading your thoughts. 'It's how the Doctor travels in space and time — how we got here.'

'And it's off limits, thanks to those guards,' hisses the Doctor, 'So I can't use anything from inside to tackle the nanobots, like I'd hoped. I'll just have to see what I can put together from stuff in the exhibition.'

You cautiously retreat to the central avenue. As you reach it, you hear footsteps approaching. Brunel comes running towards you, face flushed.

'Boilers are all up to pressure, Doctor.'

'Good man,' replies the Doctor. 'Let's see about getting a few of those machines working. It'll distract the nanobots — maybe buy me a little time to come up with a way to tackle them.'

Brunel leads you swiftly westwards until you pass under a banner reading MACHINERY IN MOTION. Ahead, several thousand square metres of floorspace are occupied by a variety of steam-powered industrial machines.

'You get started over that side,' says the Doctor to Brunel, gesturing to his left. 'We'll have a tinker with the others.'

To go with Brunel, go to 23. To go with the Doctor and Martha, go to 75.

After a mad dash past a variety of weird and wonderful exhibits, you pull up, breathless, under a banner that reads MEDIEVAL COURT.

'I think we lost him,' pants Martha.

'Let's lie low for a minute, to be on the safe side,' says the Doctor.

This area houses a collection of mock-medieval exhibits, including a gigantic Gothic-style cast iron stove. The three of you quickly squeeze behind it. Martha peers round its side, keeping watch.

'Shhhh!' she hisses. 'Someone's coming.'

You, too, can hear an approaching sound — not footsteps, but an unusual rasping sound that reminds you of someone measuring out dry rice.

'What the...' Martha sounds bewildered. 'There's some sort of black gritty stuff spilling across the floor,' she whispers. 'It's like a pool of something, only... it's dry. And it's moving like it's conscious of direction — like it's alive...'

She falls silent for a few moments, then continues, her tone even more incredulous.

'Something's forming from the black stuff. It's kind of pouring upwards from the floor, into a shape — like something melting in reverse. It's a body — a human body. I don't believe it...'

Both you and the Doctor, unable to resist, peer out too. You witness the last moments of the bizarre process — a matt black, headless human form, like an unfinished sculpture, stands in a shrinking pool of dark, sandy matter. As you watch, the pool recedes, as though sucked upwards, and the figure is completed. An instant later its entire surface changes from black to a range of colours — dark blue, brass, flesh-tone — as though suddenly illuminated. You find yourself once again looking at a Victorian police constable.

'Nanobots!' murmurs the Doctor, transfixed.

'Nanny-whats?'

'Nanobots. Tiny individual robotic units that can cooperate — like cells in a body — to create an infinite range of forms and devices.'

As you stare unbelievingly at the figure across the court, a second, uncannily identical constable strides into view and wordlessly takes up position beside the first.

'They're not policemen — they're artificial replicants, assembled from millions of microscopic robots.'

'But what are they doing here?' whispers Martha.

'Dunno.' The Doctor grins. 'Shall we ask them?'

To confront the replicant policemen, go to 56. To stay hidden, and continue to watch, go to 35.

Your efforts are in vain — the restraints hold firm. Suddenly, your eye is drawn to three pitch-black, diamond-shaped openings that hover impossibly in thin air, on the far side of the chamber. The central one is shimmering slightly. A figure steps through it — the Doctor.

'In trouble again, Miss Jones,' he smirks, crossing to help you. 'And who's your gentleman friend?' he asks, quickly releasing each of the restraints with a touch of his sonic screwdriver.

Brunel, rubbing his sore wrists, introduces himself.

The Doctor looks impressed. 'Excellent. You're one of the Exhibition's Commissioners, aren't you? Do you know how we can get some of the machinery moving? We can't fight them without some sort of power.'

'But who are "them"?' asks Martha.

'The Shryken. I should have realised the nanobots were under their control immediately. It's their standard planetary invasion strategy — send in a remote-controlled reconnaissance probe, robotically manned, to infiltrate the native population and abduct sample specimens.'

He gestures to the body-filled pod.

'They must have had their nanobots burrow beneath the Crystal Palace, assume the form of human policemen, then pick off specimens at will. The Exhibition presents an ideal sampling pool – there are folk here from all over the Earth. When the probe returns, the Shryken will analyse their biology, then custom-design a virus to wipe out the entire population. No need for conflict. Very efficient.'

'So how do we stop them?' asks Brunel.

'That's the spirit. Well, we'll need power, as I said.'

'There's a separate boiler room to the north-west of the building that feeds a system of pipes running to the heavy machinery section,' reveals Brunel. 'If I could reach the boilers, you'd have all the power you want.'

The Doctor points to the central diamond-shaped window. 'The Transmat portal I came in through opens into the railway section – that's in the north-west area…'

Brunel gives the Doctor a determined nod, strides towards the central portal, and vanishes. The Doctor turns his attention back to you and Martha.

'Now, we need to get out of here pretty sharpish, too – before we have company. Pick a portal!'

To go through the left-hand Transmat portal, go to 34. To choose the right-hand one, go to 33.

75 | Sticking close to the Doctor and Martha, you approach the largest of the nearby machines. It's a massive, steam-powered, mangle-like crushing apparatus. Its colossal steel flywheel is over four metres across. A conveyor belt feeds the giant crushing rollers.

'Sugar Cane Crushing-Mill,' Martha reads from the machine's plaque.

The Doctor is peering distractedly at another machine, some way off.

'From here that looks like some kind of hydrostatic device,' he mutters. 'Which would be very handy. You two see if you can get this beast started — I'll be back in a jiffy.'

He hurries off, leaving you and Martha to deal with the crushing-mill. But you quickly run into trouble. The machine's main steam inlet valve is stuck fast. Martha gives it a frustrated thump.

'We need something to lever it with. I'll see what I can find.'

And she too dashes away.

To continue trying to move the jammed valve, go to 64. To follow Martha, go to 54.

To the west of the locomotive section, you come to an area crowded with all shapes and sizes of horse-drawn vehicle – gigs, phaetons, barouches, and even specialised 'invalid carriages'.

'It'll be over thirty years before Benz produces the first motor car,' says the Doctor. 'This lot are the Fords and Ferraris of the moment.'

Martha is intrigued by a 'velocipede' – the nearest thing on display to a modern bicycle. It looks like a tricycle, but its twin rear wheels are powered by foot-treadles, connecting rods and a crankshaft, rather than pedals and chain.

Suddenly you notice a tall figure, in a blue top hat and tailcoat, descending the stairs from the gallery at the far end of the carriage section. You alert the Doctor, who frowns.

'Police. One of Sir Robert Peel's Metropolitan "bobbies". We'd best make ourselves scarce.'

To slip away through the neighbouring Furniture section, go to 77. To quickly hide inside one of the larger carriages, go to 38.

You pass a variety of ornate bedsteads, bookcases, wardrobes and sideboards as you move through the Furniture section. Beyond it, you come to an area with a distinctively Eastern flavour. Its exhibits include many intricate ivory carvings and richly embroidered fabrics. A colossal stuffed elephant dominates the display. It has a magnificent ivory howdah — a riding seat — on its back, topped with an elaborate canopy.

'The Indian section,' states the Doctor. 'Most of the stuff here "belongs" to the British East India Company. They've even got the famous Koh-i-Noor diamond somewhere — recently surrendered to Queen Victoria by the Maharajah of Lahore. Worth as much as all the other stuff in the Exhibition put together.'

Martha nudges you both urgently. The police constable, still on patrol, is striding your way through the Furniture section.

To duck behind the beautiful ivory throne beside you, go to 83. To run for it, go to 4.

As the creatures advance, the Doctor hurriedly takes out his sonic screwdriver. Before he can employ it in your defence, the nearest creature spits a ball of blue energy from its mouth. It hits Martha square in the chest, sending her sprawling.

The Doctor hurriedly kneels beside her, his face full of concern.

'She's alive — just stunned.'

He rises quickly to face the approaching creatures. As another stun-pulse comes fizzing your way, he lifts the sonic screwdriver. The pulse detonates in mid-air, its energy spreading outwards, as though absorbed by an invisible wall.

More projectiles rapidly follow. Although the Doctor's protective shield holds, you are driven back.

'Doctor!'

Three more replicant police constables are approaching from the other direction. You are trapped between them and the creatures. Sensing your dilemma, the creatures scuttle forward to Martha's prone body, and begin to drag her away.

To confront the constables, go to 43. To try to help Martha, go to 92.

You and Martha land safely on the four-poster's canopy. But as the Doctor leaps to join you, your combined weight proves too much for the fabric, and it tears beneath you. The three of you land in a heap on the bed below.

The Doctor bounces to his feet, beaming.

'That was fun! Let's do it again!'

The area around you is filled with wardrobes, armchairs, dining tables and more beds.

'Furniture section,' says the Doctor. 'Deeply dull. Oo — except that little gem!' He points to a nearby metal bedstead. 'The Patented Alarum Bedstead. It has a clockwork mechanism that makes its foot end collapse at a set time. Actually tips you out of bed. Brilliant.'

'Doctor! Shhh!' hisses Martha suddenly.

The police constable you narrowly avoided earlier is moving your way.

To quickly sneak across the central avenue and take the stairs signposted SILKS AND SATINS, go to 51. To keep very still and silent, in the hope that the constable will pass without noticing you, go to 59.

Splashing the Doctor's face with cold water has the desired effect — he slowly begins to come round. As you help him into a sitting position against the side of the fountain, you hear a scream from nearby. Martha has clearly regained consciousness, too.

As the Doctor immediately attempts to get to his feet, his anxious expression changes to a grimace of pain. He slumps back against the fountain, clearly still semi-paralysed by the effects of the stun-pulse.

'You need to help her,' he hisses, teeth gritted in agony. 'At least find out where they're taking her. I'll come after you as soon as I can move.'

To rush up the nearby stairs to the gallery, in the hope that you'll be able to spot Martha from there, go to 60. To hurry east along the central avenue, in the rough direction of Martha's scream, go to 46.

You pursue the nanobotic creature formed from the constable's severed arm through an area dedicated to up-to-the-minute Victorian fashion — 'Anaxyridian Trousers' that 'dispense with the need for braces'; ladies' cuffs made from 'the wool of French poodle dogs'; a range of 'Patented Ventilated Hats'.

The creature suddenly leaps at one of the many iron columns that support the great glass roof above, and scuttles up it. As it does so, the Doctor dashes quickly to the foot of the column and touches the end of his sonic screwdriver against it. The creature falls back to the floor, where it lies still.

'Electromagnetic pulse,' explains the Doctor. 'Conducted by the iron. Temporarily interferes with communication between the individual nanobots.'

To take a closer look at the stricken creature, go to 65. To hurry back and pick up the trail of the constables who seized Martha, go to 32.

You drop through the hole, falling into blackness for a few unnerving instants, before landing heavily beside the Doctor on the rock floor of a wide, underground tunnel. Eerie green light emanates from fluorescent ribs that reinforce its walls. There's no sign of the replicant policemen — or Martha.

The Doctor withdraws his sonic screwdriver and slices across the nearest wall rib in two places. He lifts away a curved section, and scrutinises it.

'It's a polymer of Zarcon.' He passes the rib to you. 'Not an element you'll find anywhere in this solar system. Whoever cut these tunnels has come a long way to see Prince Albert's Exhibition.'

Without warning, several black, football-sized spheres suddenly bowl towards you along the tunnel, coming to an abrupt halt a few metres away. They rapidly morph into a pair of multi-limbed nanobotic monstrosities.

To attempt to hold the creatures off using the tough polyzarconate tunnel rib as a weapon, go to 85. To run for it, go to 55.

As the constable passes and continues on his patrol, you emerge quietly from behind the ivory throne. Looking at it more closely, you marvel at the intricate animal carvings that decorate its pale surface.

'Bit special, isn't it?' says the Doctor. 'A gift to Queen Victoria from the Rajah of Travancore. Prince Albert will sit on it during the exhibition's closing ceremony in a few months time.'

He gives an ironic smile.

'It's gifts and tributes for Her Majesty right now, but after a few more years of British rule, the Queen can look forward to the Indian Mutiny, mass unrest, and — '

'Doctor!'

The Doctor follows Martha's pointing finger. A second police constable, top-hatted and tailcoated like the first, is wandering among the exhibits a little way off.

To creep quickly back into the furniture section, and hide inside one of the wardrobes, go to 38. To keep absolutely still and silent, in the hope that the constable will pass without noticing you, go to 59.

You step through the right-hand Transmat portal and are relieved to find yourself back in the Crystal Palace. The nearest display stand exhibits an odd-looking contraption which proudly claims to be:

CHARLES MOREY'S PATENTED SEWING MACHINE

To one side of you stands a vast piano, with a keyboard long enough for four people to play it at a time. To the other you can see several ploughs, a towering stack of milk churns, and a wide range of other agricultural exhibits, including a large horse-drawn contraption with waterwheel-like arms and paddles.

'McCormick's famous mechanical reaper. Set to change the face of farming worldwide,' states the Doctor. 'We must be in the United States section,'

Martha gives a sudden yell of warning. Several nanobotic creatures are emerging from the portal behind you.

To send the tower of milk churns toppling into their path, to slow them down, go to 72. To dash for the nearby stairway to the gallery, go to 26.

Your efforts prove futile, and both you and the Doctor are quickly taken captive by the nanobotic creatures. They forcibly escort you along a sequence of tunnels, until you arrive at a cavernous underground chamber.

'Doctor!'

Martha is here, too, guarded by a second group of creatures. You are bundled forward to join her, and the three of you are herded into a box-like cell standing against one of the chamber walls. Its door slices shut, leaving you in total darkness. Outside, you can hear the nanobotic creatures scuttling away, clearly satisfied that you are securely imprisoned.

The cell's interior is suddenly illuminated, as the Doctor activates his sonic screwdriver. By its pale blue light, you can see his excited face.

'Did you see the transparent pod at the far end of the chamber? With the people inside it, in those gel-filled capsules? Now I know who we're dealing with. The Shryken. Nasty customers. Planetary invasion is their speciality, and always using the same method. They send in a reconnaissance probe manned by robotic drones — the nanobots — to abduct a sample of the populace. When the probe returns, the Shryken study the specimens to analyse the native race's biology, then bioengineer a virus to wipe them out.'

'But why are the nanobots here, at the Great Exhibition?' asks Martha.

'It's a fantastic sampling opportunity — there are people here from all over Earth. The Shryken must have landed the remote probe nearby, then had their nanobots burrow beneath the Crystal Palace so they could take the place of the security police, as replicants, and start picking off visitors.'

His brow creases in a frown.

'I reckon that sampling pod had about fifty human specimens in it already. They must be about ready to recall the probe ship. We need to stop them.'

He runs the sonic screwdriver over the featureless, glass-like surface of the cell's door.

'But first, we need to get out of here...'

To wait while the Doctor tries to override the door's locking system, go to 52. To try to summon help, by yelling, go to 71.

You find yourself in entirely changed surroundings — a wide underground tunnel, dimly lit by the glow of fluorescent green ribs that reinforce its walls. The Doctor is beside you.

'Not one for being told, I see.' He grins at you. 'Me neither. Come on.'

You move along the tunnel, until it opens out into a vast subterranean cavern. At its centre stands a large, black, heart-shaped craft. Nanobotic creatures are scurrying busily across its smooth hull.

'That's a starship,' whispers the Doctor. 'Pretty swanky one, too.'

A stack of silver canisters stands nearby. You follow the Doctor as he crosses stealthily to it. He sniffs a canister.

'Launch propellant. I'd say they're getting her ready to fly.'

Suddenly, two of the nanobotic creatures attending to the craft begin to scuttle in your direction, carrying more of the canisters.

To attempt to hide behind the canister stack, go to 85. To run for it, go to 55.

You hurry past the carriages — sporty four-wheeler phaetons, two-wheeled gigs, soft-top cabriolets and barouches — into an area where the display stands are strewn with animal skins. There's no sign of pursuit, so you stop to catch your breath.

Draped from the gallery above are the pelts of tigers, lions, bears, and buffaloes. Feathers from ostriches and birds of paradise decorate a collection of ladies' hats. Martha, taking in a display of smaller furs labelled BLACK FOX, BEAVER and FUR SEAL, looks revolted.

'Is there anything they *didn't* kill?'

'Not much,' replies the Doctor. 'Animal rights wasn't really a nineteenth-century concept.'

Approaching footsteps bring the discussion to an end. A second police constable has responded to the rattle alarm, and is hurrying to join the chase.

To slip among the rails of furs, in the hope that the constable won't spot you, go to 59. To attempt to sneak back upstairs to the gallery and hide there, go to 5.

From your hiding place, you watch the police constable approach. He halts a few metres away, and scans the surrounding exhibits with a cold stare, as though sensing your presence. Reaching for the wooden rattle at his hip, he gives it a purposeful swirl, sending up a raucous *rata-tat-tat* alarm.

Moments later, you are puzzled to see a trickle of black powder begin to pour from the gallery above where the constable is standing, to form a pool on the floor beside him. The trickle continues, until the black, gritty pool has grown to a metre across. Then, impossibly, something begins to rise from its surface.

To your amazement, a tall, thick column quickly takes shape. As the pool of granular matter shrinks to nothing, flowing upwards to feed the growing form, it becomes recognisable as a human figure. Its surface suddenly changes from black to coloured, and a second police constable stands before you, identical in every detail to the first.

'Well I'll be... they're nanobotic!' hisses the Doctor. 'That black sandy stuff — each grain is a tiny, microscopic robotic unit — a nanobot. They can combine and cooperate in their millions to create any form they're programmed to — in this case, a replicant nineteenth-century policeman!'

To confront the nanobotic replicants, go to 56. To continue to observe them from your hiding place, go to 35.

The steam hammer is truly huge — a towering A-frame of solid metal. A gleaming piston shaft down the machine's central channel ends in a hefty hammerhead, which can clearly be driven down with great force onto the anvil below. The device's massive frame bears the name of its manufacturer:

J.NASMYTH & CO.
ENGINEERS
MANCHESTER

Beside the machine are a number of wrought iron bars that have been pummelled flat, presumably during demonstrations of the mighty forge at work.

'I'll need to open a main inlet valve,' says Brunel. 'Stay here.' And he hurries away.

As you wait, you hear an unsettling noise. A lone nanobotic creature is stalking nearby, drawn by the sound of the Applegath press.

To quickly hide behind the steam hammer's vast frame, go to 61. To confront the creature, brandishing one of the flattened iron bars, go to 63.

You follow the Doctor down to the ground floor of the vast exhibition hall. The area in which you emerge is crammed with a wide variety of tools and equipment. Some items you recognise — a basic wooden plough, for instance — while others, such as the four-legged, barrel-shaped contraption that the Doctor is admiring, are entirely unfamiliar.

'Agricultural Machines and Implements,' explains the Doctor. 'The Victorians came up with a million and one ways to use machinery and power to improve farming methods. This is an "Archimedean Root Washer", apparently. You load it with mucky potatoes, I guess. Give the handle a twizzle, and they pop out the other end nice and clean.'

He grins delightedly.

'Fabulous.'

Suddenly Martha comes charging down the stairs behind you, eyes full of alarm.

'Police!' she shrieks. 'Right behind me!'

To run for it through the Agricultural section, go to 73. To quickly hide inside a nearby hay cart, go to 88.

You hurry through the exhibition alone, in search of the telegraphic equipment, always on the lookout for your nanobotic enemies. Then, suddenly, there it is — a cabinet displaying *REID'S ELECTRIC TELEGRAPHS*.

The telegraph receivers each have one or more needle dials, showing the letters of the alphabet. You guess that the needles can be made to move, to spell out messages.

Before you can grab anything, a telltale scuttling noise sends you diving for cover. Peering from behind a cabinet, you watch a bug-like nanobotic creature approach. Its insectoid head scans from side to side, as though trying to pick up a trail. You soon realise whose, when you spot Martha moving stealthily through the exhibits a little way off, out of sight of the creature.

To stay hidden, and hope for a chance to grab the telegraph equipment, go to 61.
To follow Martha, go to 54.

You and the Doctor follow the creatures as they scuttle away with the unconscious Martha. The pursuit leads through an area displaying examples of fine European furniture. One particularly impressive item is a colossal sideboard with a vast looking-glass above it — by far the largest mirror you have ever seen.

To your astonishment, the creatures, without slowing their scuttling run, launch themselves at this giant mirror, and pass impossibly through it.

'Transmat portal!' yells the Doctor, streaking ahead of you. Without breaking stride, he too leaps on to the sideboard and vanishes through the surface of the mirror. Incredulously, you follow suit.

You find yourself in a dimly-lit, gently sloping, rock-walled tunnel. Eerie green light comes from bands of fluorescent resin that rib the walls at intervals. The creatures — and Martha — are nowhere to be seen.

To follow the downward-slope of the tunnel, go to 29. To take the opposite direction, go to 19.

'I *love* this section!' enthuses the Doctor, happily browsing the wacky-looking gadgets that fill the Philosophical Instruments gallery. 'It's all the stuff they couldn't easily classify — early electrical devices and off-the-wall scientific inventions.'

'Right up your street, then,' smirks Martha.

Ignoring her, the Doctor shepherds you towards a large dome-shaped device.

'Look at this gem — the Tempest Prognosticator. It's a weather forecasting machine. See the squiggly black things in the glass chambers around the bottom? They're leeches. There's a tiny chain running from the neck of each leech chamber, to the bell at the top. The chap who came up with this — a Dr Merryweather, no less — knew that leeches get agitated when there's a storm brewing. When the leeches get fidgety, their movements jiggle the chains, which activate tiny hammers around the central bell. They set it ringing, forecasting bad weather. Brilliant. Absolutely bonkers, but brilliant.'

To continue browsing the Philosophical Instruments, go to 16. To move further along the gallery, turn to page 41.

You hold your breath, crouched behind the giant ship's engine. Slowly, the constable's footsteps recede.

'Coast's clear!' beams the Doctor, emerging. 'I was telling you about Victorian steam ships. Most are British — Britannia rules the waves, and all that. There was a model of one of the Royal Navy's fastest steamers up in the gallery — HMS *Medea.*'

He lowers his voice dramatically.

'And do you know what the *Medea* brought back from India on her most recent voyage?'

You shake your head.

'The Koh-i-Noor. Mountain of Light. One of the world's largest diamonds. Displayed just over...' — he points eastward along the nave — 'there.'

Martha makes a disparaging noise. 'A diamond's a diamond, I'm not big on jewellery.' She points to a banner over the nearby staircase. 'I'd rather take a peek at Silks and Satins upstairs.'

'Fair enough,' shrugs the Doctor. 'Why don't we let our young friend choose?'

To go upstairs to the textile gallery, go to 51. To see the Koh-i-Noor, go to 22.

Step into a world of wonder and mystery with Sarah Jane and her gang in:

1. Invasion of the Bane
2. Revenge of the Slitheen
3. Eye of the Gorgon
4. Warriors of the Kudlak

And don't miss these other exciting adventures with the Doctor!

1. The Spaceship Graveyard
2. Alien Arena
3. The Time Crocodile
4. The Corinthian Project
5. The Crystal Snare
6. War of the Robots
7. Dark Planet
8. The Haunted Wagon Train